Jasper's Birth[...]

Written by Michèle Dufresne · Illustrated by Sterling Lamet

Pioneer Valley Educational Press, Inc.

Today is Jasper's birthday.

"Where is Jasper?" said Tony.

"He's hiding under my bed," said Katie. "I can't get him to come out for his birthday party."

3

"I have a birthday present for Jasper," said Tony. "Scruffy has a birthday present, too."

"Jasper likes presents," said Katie.

"We can show him the birthday presents."

Katie and Tony and Scruffy went upstairs.

"Look, Jasper," said Katie.
"Here are some
birthday presents for you.
Please come out!"

Jasper looked
at the presents
but he did not come out.

Katie and Tony and Scruffy
went downstairs.
"Mom," said Katie.
"Jasper is hiding
under my bed.
It's time for his party!"

"Hmmm," said Mom.

11

"Look, Jasper," said Mom.
"Here is your birthday cake.
It's a tuna cake!"